HALF MOON
TONITE

SONIA A. HURALECZKO

HALF MOON
TONITE

SONIA HURALECZKO

WORKBOOK PRESS LLC
187 E Warm Springs Rd,
Suite B285, Las Vegas, NV 89119, USA

Website: https://workbookpress.com/
Hotline: 1-888-818-4856
Email: admin@workbookpress.com

Ordering Information:
Quantity sales. Special discounts are available on quantity purchases by cor-
porations, associations, and others. For details, contact the publisher at the
address above.

Library of Congress Control Number:
ISBN-13:   978-1-952754-30-2(Paperback Version)
                                      978-1-952754-40-1(Digital Version)

REV. DATE: 10/06/2020

CONTENTS

The Statue of Liberty · 01

A Perfect Day · 02

More than Ever · 03

Pretty in Pink · 04

I'll Never Forget You · 06

I'm Just Hangin' On · 07

Faith · 08

The Medallion · 09

KING OF KINGS · 10

From Heaven Above · 11

Half Moon Tonite · 12

Butterfly Pictures · 13

Bee in the Screen · 14

What a Disorder · 15

The Bench · 16

A Handsome Man · 18

Oh Sweet Jesus, I Pray · 19

Happy Birthday, MaMa · 20

The Window Sill · 21

The Brisk Morning · 22

Tea, Honey, and Milk · 23

America's Pastime · 24

Homeless · 25

Why, GOD? · 27

<u>PART II</u>

What Can I Give To This Lady 29

In The Arms Of Jesus 31

Violence 2017 32

A Ray Of Hope 33

Thankful Things 34

O, Sweet Jesus I Pray 35

Oh, How I Miss My Mother 36

In The Stillness Of The Night 37

God Only Knows How Much I Loved You 38

I'll Get By 39

Prayer Gives Light 40

The Stars Were So Bright 41

Through The Woods 42

The Children Of Africa 43

The Statue of Liberty

There are a lot of things that are wrong
But we have to make them right
If we could maybe sing a song
Maybe the world would look more bright

So many wars at hand
In my opinion, we should take a stand
But our soldiers die every day,
Is this the real way?

Is freedom not free
As our beautiful flag waves
With peace in the air
For all of us to share

People from all over come here
To see our Statue of Liberty stand
And soldiers die everyday
Is this really the real way

Freedom is not free
And our beautiful flag does wave
For all to share peace in the air
I think it does seem fair

May God Bless this country
As He always has
With peace and prosperity
That comes across this land.

A Perfect Day

It's Sunday today
And the birds and the squirrels are
Already at play
In the morning, where the grass is green
A sight to behold and unseen.

You don't need a magnifying glass to see
The beauty of what God gave for me
A place to stay
And a beautiful window where I can pray.
I don't have to be anywhere but here
But only with the morning rays that are
So near
It would be nice to have someone close
To my heart
To finally let go and have then have it start

It's Sunday today
In the morningwhere the grass is green
A sight to behold and unseen.

More than Ever

Oh, how I wish you were here
When the mist on the grass in the mornin'
We would walk with the sun risin'
And cross the forest through the streams

Splash over our faces with fresh spring water
And walk with our footsteps on rocks together
With the mountains moving within us forever
It seems as though I feel for you more than ever.

With God shining on us with warmth and glory
He might say as He looks upon us
We are the perfect spiritual couple
And would give us His promise.

Pretty in Pink

We wonder how were going to make it
Our paycheck just doesn't seem to break it
We squander around all month long
We try so hard just to belong

Mama's sitting there watching T.V.
Wondering what to make for me
Papa's all gone, what a shame
But who is there going to blame

Proud Papa's is down Chestnut Street
Where people live to drink and eat
Give me that pasta bowtie anytime
Only out of my pocket, a quarter and a dime

My credit card is so high that I could almost cry
But these are a new pair of shoes which makes
My eyes dry
My shoes are all pretty in pink
And now I can walk in the park and think

My car is in the Florida dump
So, I have nothing to use at the pump
But, Jack, at the gas station will do me a fax
So, I can get a job and finally relax

My nephew, Andy, is so young and strong
He's finishing college and it won't be long
He has a band that sings rock-n-roll
And all he has to do is break the mole

Steven is a regular guy who likes a drink
He says it's better this way to think
He works at a diner all hours of the day
Trying to make it thru the light of day

We wonder how we're going to make
Our paycheck just doesn't seem to break it.

I'll Never Forget You

Shedding layers and layers of feelings
How I try to get to the core of my heart
And end up wanting more

Getting to know myself was no mere task
I think, all my life, I've been wearing a mask
The pain is going away
Sometimes I dreamed that you could have
Stayed

The light in your eyes will always be with me
And in my heart and spirit, too
I learned so many things
As I shed these layers in two.

Before I go on, I wish I could tell you
That there's no one to blame
And that I will always love you
And never forget you in shame

Maybe I'll see you on another plane
With no layers and layers to shed
I'll leave you with this note
And bless you with all the most.

Im Just Hangin' On

Being in love for me was short-lived
I wish I could catch it.
I'm just hangin' on a string.

But at least I was in love once
Some people don't even know what
Loves means
I've gone with so much time dreamin'
And I'm becoming weary.

Is it time to move on to someone else?
Or time to move for myself;
I get so caught up in it
I end up losing myself.

I haven't been praying lately
But I'm going to now
Just one more time and ask Jesus
To bring my husband around

I'll wait and see one more time again,
Dream, write, and rhyme again
And pray again.

Faith

I feel solemn today
Maybe I'll go out and pray
To a church full of joy and song
Some place where I can belong

The rain is drizzling a little
And maybe I'll fit in the crowd in
The middle
So, I'll step out to this place
And, slowly lose this wretched face.

What is it that is in store for me
In this place that is all charity free
And as I look up to the sky
And question my true demise

I hope I will find my answers in time
And not only believe in this little rhyme
But abound to real true faith
As the preachers always do sayeth.

I felt solemn today
Maybe I'll out and pray
To a church full of joy and song
Some place where I can belong.

The Medallion

I lost a medallion one day
From my hands it drifted away
I have tears falling down my face
As I lost my favorite jewel
In that wretched place!

It was all of gold and engraved
With a beauty that was a sight to behold
How I miss this piece of treasure
How I prayed to God for it's return;
It gave me so much pleasure!

This medallion was no regular treasure
It was one of Mary and Baby Jesus
It lifted my spirit beyond measure

But, alas, one day I was crossing the park
And lo' and behold I saw a sign, a mark
Another medallion of Mary and Jesus to wear
Around my neck!

This time I won't lose this sacred heart
But keep it close to my heart
It's a nice day today!
Right around the Christmas Holiday!

Kings Of Kings

In my own imagination
In my own hallucination
There's a man on a horse
Who is set on a fine coarse

The path is narrow but yet great
It's not only that it will be by fate
But a spirit full of faith
In which we could bathe

The man on the horse wears a
Cape and crown
And it's highly unlikely the colors
Are of brown But of rubies, emeralds, diamonds
On gold
Only one crown that breaks all molds

I have been fighting the evil spirits
Of the world Now
I'm tired and going back to the Lord
So, it's up to you to take care and
I'll be praying for you down there.

I am the "King of Kings"
And I will rule one day
I will come with a sword and rod
On my white horse I will jump and trod.

The man on the white horse wears a cape and crown . . .

From Heaven Above

He came to me in a dream
Slowly and gently walking
Towards our bed so wide
He looked at me and laid there
As he put his hand on my side

He was dressed in white
With eyes which stared so bright
A smile as good as any gold
I think he really broke the mold

He called my name
And I turned away like a willow
+He called again
And turned to him from my pillow

How tender it was to feel his kiss
He gave on that very night
And how it felt so real
And how it felt so right

Is it a sign from heaven above
Telling us were one
Is it a blessing from above
Where heavenly spirits have shown.

Half Moon Tonite

Half moon tonite and you're so far away
Can you ever forgive me
Please, come back home someday

You've made me your Babe and honestly
I could say
I love you over each and everyday

You say, Babe, don't trust the world
And your right
But don't forget, she can also be very
Very bright

You've given me my world back to me
I've never flown
And I feel like a little child
Who has finally just grown

Half moon tonite and you're so far away . . .

Butterfly Pictures

I have butterflies with purple flowers on my door
I have little butterfly pots on my sill
I have a butterfly bracelet on my wrist
And butterflies after the mist

I've known you in my heart for quite sometime
And I'd never thought I'd be able to rhyme
And these butterflies in my heart
Have given me thoughts of time

Butterflies fly so freely; I wonder why it makes
Them so
Has God intended it to be that way
All year long I wish they could stay

I have butterfly pictures in these letters
I couldn't understand why
But now I feel and see that butterflies
Are free to fly.

Bee in the Screen

Bee in the screen
Don't know how it got there
Near a corner where prayers were said
Where marks on the furnace
Were once was bred

He stared at the ceiling
Where it aimed so high
He was thinking of God
And gave him a great big nod

Near the window he looked at
The moon and the stars
Fell to his knees and with tears in
His eyes
And gazed towards the blue skies

As he fell to the ground
He made no sound
Then, cried out loud and
Imagined "The Shroud"

He went back to bed with
The bee in the screen
And fell asleep
And did no longer weep.

What A Disorder

Remembering Van Gogh when he cut his ear
That is something that I would fear
You see, I am the same
And there is no one to blame

I was born with such an order
I hope I'll never end up like a martyr
But live a life that is full at 50
And learn to be a little more thrifty

I see the world with babes' eyes
And it is everybody's real demise
To see what I see
Always looking at the world with glee

It took a long time to get well
Although, I always did hear the
Churches bells
And with the world as it stands
I think I can bear it's hands

One day, I hope to offer my good ways
And I think I will get much praise
As I once wrote poems well-liked
I really think I can get well psyched.

The Bench

The bench, the bench is a place of
listening and giving
Where people come and go
To adorn their style of living

Here comes Ted in the morning
with his hair all straight and tidy
Looking ready to take a smoke
But all he could do is choke

Then comes Sam, the macho man
with Babe leashed on his right hand
Some people wish they can walk little Babe
But what you get is a great big maybe

There comes Dell, the beautiful Italian lady
Who will never ask for a smoke
But instead she'll sit there 'till doomsday
Until she goes up in smoke

We'll never forget Frank, who sat
at the corner of the bench
He looked like a Mafia guy
And wore a brimmed hat and stenchy trench
We'll never forget Frank!

The wars play a part at Ehrhart Gardens
Luba, Bud, Danny and Steve live

Freely now
It's not a funny thing
That once they sacrificed their lives therein.

And last but not least, there's Don
Who was in rehab for 90 days
God only knows how he got there
And tells the same story on many days

The bench is a place of listening and giving . . .

A Handsome Man

Walking to the store with my carriage
In the midst, thinking of my marriage.

How we blossomed once
As it lasted a year and a few months

He was a handsome man from Turkey
Who never made life merky.

He traveled the world so far
And, occasionally, sat at the bar.

He was a religious man
Who always did make a stand

He was like a squirrel in the grass
And leaped, oh, so fast.

You see, he was a man of different faith
As he always did sayeth.

Walking to the store with my carriage
In the midst, thinking of my marriage.

Oh Sweet Jesus, I Pray

O, Sweet Jesus, why is it so hard
When you love someone so much
And the hand gives you a bad card

I loved this man with all my heart
And all I could do is cry
Because he is so far away.

Please, Sweet Jesus, bring him back to me
So our souls will be set free
Together, in love
A blessing from heaven above …

He is so far away, and all I can do is pray
That maybe in heaven, we will be
Forever, together, him and me.

Happy Birthday, MaMa

I have nothing in my pocket
And I can't get you a locket
But, at this day, I'll be oh, so, kind
And give you a little peace of mind

Birthdays come and go
And I want to make this special
Because you are so dear
and it is essential

I love you with all my heart
Because you are so very smart
And on this day we celebrate
And I'll hold my tongue and not
To berrate

Please forgive me of my faults
And I think I'm going to exhault
So pick me up and let me know
Forever more we will grow

I

The Window Sill

Where plastic plant butterflies sitting
On the window sill
And a clock is running until

A jewelry box with precious small
Treasures
And a card from a special person
Put in with pleasures

Crystal candles adorn the sill
While tea lights light
As the clock runs till

An angel of gratefulness in
Another spot
Sitting proudly displayed near
A planted pot

With Jesus in the middle
Raising his hands
For all to see
His sacred heart for free

A squirrel in a picture
Reminding me of you
Holding a daisy and saying
"I love you."

The Brisk Morning

The geese in the field are quietly sitting
And mom's in the other room knitting her knitting
Anxiously waiting for the Christmas Tree fitting

The morning is so brisk
And to go outside is of little risk
I'll go out and feel the chill of the air
Instead of sitting in this old chair

As I'm walking through the streets
It is of no great feat
But a mere simple task
Where no one wears a mask

It's almost Christmas time in 30 days
And feel already it's Christmas
I love this time of year
It doesn't bring any fear

Let's take a moment and enjoy
Breathe the fresh air
Because it is so rare.

Tea, Honey, and Milk

Tea, honey, and milk
Is all due to the feeling of silk
I cozy on up into the arms of
An antique chair
And lose all my care

The honey is so very sweet
That I'm just about ready to tweet
Another sip I will take
And all will fall into place –
For goodness sake!

The tea is so delightfully warming
Unlike coffee which is quite
Alarming love to lounge sipping
My tea
Because it puts me in a state
Of glee!

America's Pastime

Money goin' in, money goin' out
Time goin' in, time goin' out
We make our money to pay our bills
And celebrate a little

We like to sit at a concert and listen
To the fiddle
We go to a baseball game and sit in the
Middle
And burgers and hot dogs grilling
On the griddle

I lost my keys today pushing a Vietnam
Vet
We found a graciousness when we met
We talked about the presidents and we bet
that the world would look like a
Shakespeare's set

These cigarettes we smoked are long gone
Now people are using marijuana in a bong
Sometimes I wish I could go along
But my medicine helps keep me strong

So much time on my hands . . .
But as time has it . . .
I salute the vet who stands like a man.

Homeless

As I walked along the Florida beaches
And swam the ocean under the moon-lit sky
I felt a peace deep inside of me
And no longer felt the need to cry

I came from Jersey
Where life can be quite quick and slick
A place of action;
A place full of attraction

I took my car and drove and drove
On Interstate-95
Till I reached my destination.
How I longed for that beautiful
Orange sky and to never say goodbye

As I lay on the beach a girl approaches
She gives me a knapsack of food and clothing
How sweet it was of her to lend a hand
As if our Lord gave her a spiritual command

I walked and walked until blisters came abound
the cops had me – had me times three
And to get a glass of water was such a big bother.
I wish I never came here; I was thinking of my
mother

It wasn't a pretty picture
An experience I'll never forget

But bless the little girl,
Who filled my life with drink

This poem is not meant for money
But to wish the homeless the strength to pursue
So, one day, I wish, you can buy some sweet
honey
With a pocket full of money.

Why, GOD?

As I listen to these Ukrainian Christmas songs
All of a sudden, I feel a sense I belong

I wonder how it is on the other side
As soldiers lay down their lives for a fight

Why God, is their bloodshed spilled all over
The ground
Where the echo, in my mind, of the bombs
Make my light heart pound

A sound I don't want to hear
A sound that's full of dread and fear

Why God, must bloodshed be?
For justice, humanity, and to be free?

Where righteousness follows
God blesses the righteous as God allows.

Part 2

What Can I give To This Lady

I think a puzzle I'll give her
And bingo we'll play after dinner
And maybe play cards on the table
And hopefully, make her feel more stable.

She's a lady with some troubles
Her life is beginning to crumble
Oh, how I wish I could help her
Where diamonds and furs can't help her.

She'd like to see her children more often,
Where her heart would be more softened.
Oh, how I wish I can help her
Where everything's such a blur.

She thinks of her husband whom she loved
So much,
And photographs of him displayed as such;
Memories long gone by,
As she reflects with a sigh.

I hope I can help this lady
And I'm not one to be shady
But I want to help as much as I can
So, we don 't fall into the quicksand.

She has an illness that I don't want to disclose
For she might feel offended with a prose.
For all I hope is to give her some soothing
And hope it will be quite moving.

She stares at photographs through the course
Of the day,
And even if she can't remember the months of
September and May,
I"ll keep her through the light of day.

In The Arms of Jesus

I can see Jesus embracing him with open arms
How he feels the warmth and tenderness he longed.
Looking into His eyes; he sees His sweet embrace.
Oh, how I wish I was in his place.

For Jesus loves all of us more than we can ever dream,
And holds us in the highest of esteem,
I know I will see Him one day,
As my brother is in His arms to stay...Forever and Ever.

Violence 2017

And God said, "THOU SHALT NOT KILL"
Taking a life seems to be a thrill
But you can get thrills anywhere
It just isn't fair.

I'll keep my oath, as we all should
I wish we all would.
I pray every day for world peace
I hope the wars would finally cease.

And today, I see another war
In our own country, not from afar.
I ask God for bloodshed to stop
I dread if I ever heard a pop-pop.

Please God, look upon us
Tell us what to do.
You engraved in stone,
"THOU SHALT NOT KILL"
Taking a life is no mere thrill.

A Ray Of Hope

Her mental and emotional stance were stripped
And her spiritual well-being lost her grip.
This little girl lost everything she had
And her mind was about to go very mad.

She is full of fears
And no one would ever sneer,
Her spirit was virtuously lost,
And as such, at a very high cost.

In older years, she went to get help
And after many years the medicines finally
Did help.
But she needed a reason to live
And God was the answer from whom He
Could give.

She found faith, happiness and love
From the One Man, from God above.
She will finally live in peace
As her wars had finally did cease.

I thank God for the gifts and blessings
Bestowed on this little girl,
For her heart is light and free now.
She goes to church to kneel and bow,
Before our Lord, she keeps her vow.
Her fears disappeared and made her stronger;

And as such, made her life live longer.
She praises God for her life from above,
Without any heartaches and a spirit full of
Love.

Thankful Things

I want to thank God for the pair of shoes on my feet
There are so many brothers and sisters who have barefeet.

I have thanks to God for the pretty blouse on my back
Instead of wearing a torn scorned sack.

I want to thank God for medications that I take
For they keep me whole, " for goodness sake!"

I want to thank God for churches, mosques, and synagogues,
For they teach me how to understand and pray
And as not to go astray.

I want to thank God for family and friends,
Because they always make my heart mend.

I want to thank God for where we are,
Where you are safe and sound and not somewhere
From afar.

I thank God for our flag as she bears the stars
and stripes,
And protects us in our land.

But most of all, and not least,
I thank God for my little Candy girl,
Who keeps me warm at night,
She is such a pearl.

O, Sweet Jesus I pray

O, sweet Jesus, I pray,
Sometimes I don't know what to say.
But maybe just to give me some strength
And make my light little heart mend,
And to see the world with Your heart and
Eyes,
So, as not to fill my heart with cries.
I know You will come through for me,
And let my little heart become free.
Please, sweet Jesus, embrace and protect me,
For you are the One, Who can only save me.

Oh, How I Miss My Mother

My auntie had a dream one night
And, it was of not of any fright
But an awakening of some kind
For which she hoped she could find.

You see, my brother had appeared to her,
And said, "I miss my mother."
Now some feel dreams are true
And some feel dreams are construed.

My mother heard the words from
My auntie's lips
On how my brother misses his mother.
She cried like a baby all night long –
How she wanted to embrace him
And sing Him a sweet lullaby song.

I wish I could see my brother...
Maybe one day in a dream...

In The Stillness Of The Night

The white, clear moon with its deep purple haze
Puts my mind at a glaze
With its majestic colors and clouds circling around
It's no wonder there is no sound.

The wet snow heavily adorning the green pine trees
The remarkable snow fascinating the moon
Reflections of colors of pink, purple, and red
And there was nothing said.

Full moon tonight
She's there with all her might
No need to be afraid and don't lose her sight
She comes and goes at full flight.

Snow, the snow with reflections of purple and red!
In the stillness of the night!
I feel I can breathe the fresh crisp air
And it all comes together and seems oh, so, fair.

God Only Knows How Much I Loved You

Raindrops on my window
Leaves my heart in tears
Raindrops in my eyes
My heart in full demise

I thought we'd come through
Once more
But as fate has said it
We are none forevermore

I thought maybe we'd win with a fight
And together make a stance
God only knows how much I loved you
I thought maybe we had one more chance

Maybe I should have shown more
Maybe our hearts would have soared
Raindrops on my windowpane
How I wish I was in your arms again

I'll Get By

I'll get by because I have shoes on my feet
With sandals and flip flops and sneakers and
No bare feet.

I'll get by with my Buick car and go to far away
places where I can become a shooting star.

I'll get by with my beautiful home
This is where the seeds have been sown.

I'll get by with the friends I possess
They are the ones that create such a mess.

I'll get by with the coins in my pocket
And go to the five and dime and buy
A locket.

I'll get by with writing poems
And in the morning read the poetic
Psalms.

I'll get by on prayers to the Man above
And go about singing like a spiritual dove.

Prayers Gives Light

I encourage you to actively pray
For what is there more to say
But to bring your heart to a High
Power,
And feel like a beautiful precious
flower.

The need to pray is universal
And can be quite controversial
So, please pray for yourselves and
Everywhere you go,
And stand and shine; for you will glow.

Miracles do happen with prayer and
Meditation
And sometimes beats a great vacation.
So, please, please, pray
And your hearts will never dismay.

The Stars Were So Bright

As I lay on the floor
I ended up wanting more.
This feeling of peace...
I hoped would never cease.

It was a surreal and euphoric feeling
One I'll never forget.
How I was in heaven almost
And how we almost met.

The stars were so bright and so near
That it was so surreal.
The angels alongside; floating not to
collide.

The tunnel was vast and then went narrow,
At the end was a strong beautiful light
Where I didn't feel the need to fight.

I was then awoken, it wasn't my time yet
To finally hear the unspoken
For which I do regret.

I have another chance and hope to make
a stance,
For this new poem that I own
I hope I've planted the seeds I've sown.

The stars were so bright...
The angels alongside...

Through The Woods

In my own imagination, in my own hallucination
There is a man on a white horse who is set on a
very fine coarse.

He and the white horse are moving so swiftly,
I can't understand why: He is trying to fight
Evil : He must move very quickly.

Through the woods where the mountains are,
It must be where winter is not so from afar.
The leaves are full of flavorful, crushing sounds
And hooves of the horse are moving abound.

His white cape is overflowing with madness,
And my heart sees Him with gladness,
He is trying to save the earth
Because it is of well worth.

The wind is moving against Him,
And it looks so very glim,
I wish I could save Him,
But He is not One to be saved.

His sacred sword has been unleashed,
His Divine Spirit through the woods has
Been preached.
The moral of the story is to see
The life of a virtuous Man born to thee.

The Children of Africa

"Food and love" the lady says,
Are what her children need.

The rounded small bowls of potted clay
Are what is needed for her to feed.

Her love is strong and goes a long way,
But what she can't get is food today.

Twenty million will go hungry this year,
A number that I dread and fear.

Prayers are well and good,
But, people can help if they only
Would.

So, open your eyes and look
Around,
And see the lost children you
Have found.

www.ingramcontent.com/pod-product-compliance
Lightning Source LLC
Chambersburg PA
CBHW071842190726
48292CB00005B/1886